The Unexpected

Jack London

first published in

1907

It is a simple matter to see the obvious, to do the expected. The tendency of the individual life is to be static rather than dynamic, and this tendency is made into a propulsion by civilization, where the obvious only is seen, and the unexpected rarely happens. When the unexpected does happen, however, and when it is of sufficiently grave import, the unfit perish. They do not see what is not obvious, are unable to do the unexpected, are incapable of adjusting their well-grooved lives to other and strange grooves. In short, when they come to the end of their own groove, they die.

On the other hand, there are those that make toward survival, the fit individuals who escape from the rule of the obvious and the expected and adjust their lives to no matter what strange grooves they may stray into, or into which they may be forced. Such an individual was Edith Whittlesey. She was born in a rural district of England, where life proceeds by rule of thumb and the unexpected is so very unexpected that when it happens it is looked upon as an immorality. She went into service early, and while yet a young woman, by rule-of-thumb progression, she became a lady's maid.

The effect of civilization is to impose human law upon environment until it becomes machine-like in its regularity. The objectionable is eliminated, the inevitable is foreseen. One is not even made wet by the rain nor cold by the frost; while death, instead of stalking about grewsome and accidental, becomes a prearranged pageant, moving along a well-oiled groove to the family vault, where the hinges are kept from rusting and the dust from the air is swept continually away.

Such was the environment of Edith Whittlesey. Nothing happened. It could scarcely be called a

happening, when, at
the age of twenty-
five, she accompanied
her mistress on
a bit of travel to
the United States.
The groove merely
changed its direction.
It was still the same
groove and well oiled.
It was a groove that
bridged the Atlantic
with uneventfulness,
so that the ship was
not a ship in the
midst of the sea,

but a capacious,
many-corridored
hotel that moved
swiftly and placidly,
crushing the waves
into submission
with its colossal
bulk until the sea
was a mill-pond,
monotonous with
quietude. And at
the other side the
groove continued
on over the land—a
well-disposed,
respectable groove

that supplied hotels at every stopping-place, and hotels on wheels between the stopping-places.

In Chicago, while her mistress saw one side of social life, Edith Whittlesey saw another side; and when she left her lady's service and became Edith Nelson, she betrayed, perhaps faintly, her ability to grapple with the unexpected and to master it. Hans Nelson, immigrant, Swede by birth and carpenter by occupation, had in him that Teutonic unrest that drives the race ever westward on its great adventure. He was a large-muscled, stolid sort of a man, in whom little imagination was coupled with immense initiative, and who possessed, withal, loyalty and affection as sturdy as his own strength.

"When I have worked hard and saved me some money, I will go to Colorado," he had told Edith on the day after their wedding. A year later they were in Colorado, where Hans Nelson

saw his first mining
and caught the
mining-fever himself.
His prospecting led
him through the
Dakotas, Idaho, and
eastern Oregon, and
on into the mountains
of British Columbia.
In camp and on trail,
Edith Nelson was
always with him,
sharing his luck, his
hardship, and his toil.
The short step of the
house-reared woman

she exchanged for the long stride of the mountaineer. She learned to look upon danger clear-eyed and with understanding, losing forever that panic fear which is bred of ignorance and which afflicts the city-reared, making them as silly as silly horses, so that they await fate in frozen horror instead of grappling with it, or stampede in blind self-destroying terror which clutters the way with their crushed carcasses.

Edith Nelson met the unexpected at every turn of the trail, and she trained her vision so that she saw in the landscape, not the obvious, but the concealed. She, who had never cooked in her life, learned to make bread without the mediation of hops, yeast, or baking-powder, and to bake bread, top and bottom, in a frying-pan before an open fire. And when the last cup of flour was gone and the last rind of bacon, she was able to rise to the occasion, and of moccasins and the softer-tanned

bits of leather in
the outfit to make a
grub-stake substitute
that somehow held
a man's soul in his
body and enabled
him to stagger on.
She learned to pack
a horse as well as
a man,—a task to
break the heart and
the pride of any
city-dweller, and she
knew how to throw
the hitch best suited
for any particular

kind of pack. Also, she could build a fire of wet wood in a downpour of rain and not lose her temper. In short, in all its guises she mastered the unexpected. But the Great Unexpected was yet to come into her life and put its test upon her.

The gold-seeking tide was flooding

northward into Alaska, and it was inevitable that Hans Nelson and his wife should he caught up by the stream and swept toward the Klondike. The fall of 1897 found them at Dyea, but without the money to carry an outfit across Chilcoot Pass and float it down to Dawson. So Hans Nelson worked at his trade that winter and helped rear the mushroom outfitting-town of Skaguay.

He was on the edge of things, and throughout the winter he heard all Alaska calling to him. Latuya Bay called loudest, so that the summer of 1898 found him and his wife threading the mazes of the broken coast-line in seventy-foot Siwash canoes. With them were Indians, also three other men. The Indians landed them and their supplies in a lonely bight of land a hundred miles or so beyond Latuya Bay, and returned to Skaguay; but the three other men remained, for they were members of the organized party. Each had put an equal share of capital into the outfitting, and the profits were to be divided equally. In that Edith Nelson undertook to cook for the outfit, a man's share was to be her portion.

First, spruce trees were cut down and a three-room cabin constructed. To keep this cabin was Edith Nelson's task. The task of the men was to search for gold, which they did; and to find gold, which they likewise did. It was not a startling find, merely a low-pay placer where long hours of severe toil earned each man between fifteen and twenty dollars a day. The brief Alaskan summer protracted itself beyond its usual length, and they took advantage of the opportunity, delaying their return to Skaguay to the last moment. And then it was too late. Arrangements had been made to accompany the several dozen local Indians on their fall trading trip down the coast. The Siwashes had waited on the white people until the eleventh hour, and then departed. There was no course left the party but to wait for chance transportation. In the meantime the claim was cleaned up and firewood stocked in.

The Indian summer had dreamed on and on, and then, suddenly, with the sharpness of bugles, winter came. It came in a single night, and the miners awoke to howling wind, driving snow, and freezing water. Storm followed storm, and between the storms there was the silence, broken only by the boom of the surf on the desolate shore, where the salt spray rimmed the beach with frozen white.

All went well in the cabin. Their gold-dust

had weighed up something like eight thousand dollars, and they could not but be contented. The men made snowshoes, hunted fresh meat for the larder, and in the long evenings played endless games of whist and pedro. Now that the mining had ceased, Edith Nelson turned over the fire-building and the dish-washing to the men, while she darned their socks and mended their clothes.

There was no grumbling, no bickering, nor petty quarrelling in the little cabin, and they often congratulated one another on the general happiness of the party. Hans Nelson was stolid and easy-going, while

Edith had long before won his unbounded admiration by her capacity for getting on with people. Harkey, a long, lank Texan, was unusually friendly for one with a saturnine disposition, and, as long as his theory that gold grew was not challenged, was quite companionable. The fourth member of the party, Michael

Dennin, contributed his Irish wit to the gayety of the cabin. He was a large, powerful man, prone to sudden rushes of anger over little things, and of unfailing good-humor under the stress and strain of big things. The fifth and last member, Dutchy, was the willing butt of the party. He even went out of his way

to raise a laugh at
his own expense
in order to keep
things cheerful. His
deliberate aim in life
seemed to be that of
a maker of laughter.
No serious quarrel
had ever vexed the
serenity of the party;
and, now that each
had sixteen hundred
dollars to show for a
short summer's work,
there reigned the

well-fed, contented spirit of prosperity.

And then the unexpected happened. They had just sat down to the breakfast table. Though it was already eight o'clock (late breakfasts had followed naturally upon cessation of the steady work at mining) a candle in the neck of a bottle lighted the meal. Edith and Hans sat at each end of the table. On one side, with their backs to the door, sat Harkey and Dutchy. The place on the other side was vacant. Dennin had not yet come in.

Hans Nelson looked at the empty chair, shook his head slowly, and, with a ponderous attempt at humor, said: “Always is he first at the grub. It is very strange. Maybe he is sick.”

“Where is Michael?” Edith asked.

“Got up a little ahead of us and went outside,” Harkey answered.

Dutchy’s face beamed mischievously. He pretended knowledge

of Dennin's absence, and affected a mysterious air, while they clamored for information. Edith, after a peep into the men's bunk-room, returned to the table. Hans looked at her, and she shook her head.

"He was never late at meal-time before," she remarked.

"I cannot understand," said Hans. "Always has he the great appetite like the horse."

"It is too bad," Dutchy said, with a sad shake of his head.

They were beginning to make merry over their comrade's absence.

"It is a great pity!" Dutchy volunteered.

"What?" they demanded in chorus.

"Poor Michael," was the mournful reply.

"Well, what's wrong with Michael?" Harkey asked.

"He is not hungry no more," wailed Dutchy. "He has lost der

appetite. He do not like der grub."

"Not from the way he pitches into it up to his ears," remarked Harkey.

"He does dot shust to be politeful to Mrs. Nelson," was Dutchy's quick retort. "I know, I know, and it is too pad. Why is he not here? Pecause he haf gone out. Why haf he gone out? For der defelopment of der appetite. How does he defelop der appetite? He walks barefoots in der snow. Ach! don't I know? It is der way der rich peoples chases after der appetite when it is no more and is running away. Michael haf sixteen hundred dollars. He is rich peoples. He haf no appetite. Derefore, pecause, he is chasing der appetite. Shust you open der door und you will see his barefoots in der snow. No, you will not see der appetite. Dot is shust his trouble. When he sees der appetite he will catch it und come to preak-fast."

They burst into loud laughter at Dutchy's nonsense. The sound

had scarcely died away when the door opened and Dennin came in. All turned to look at him.
He was carrying a shot-gun. Even as they looked, he lifted it to his shoulder and fired twice. At the first shot Dutchy sank upon the table, overturning his mug of coffee, his yellow mop of hair dabbling in his plate of mush.

His forehead, which pressed upon the near edge of the plate, tilted the plate up against his hair at an angle of forty-five degrees. Harkey was in the air, in his spring to his feet, at the second shot, and he pitched face down upon the floor, his “My God!” gurgling and dying in his throat.

It was the unexpected. Hans and Edith were stunned. They sat at the table with bodies tense, their eyes fixed in a fascinated gaze upon the murderer. Dimly they saw him through the smoke of the powder, and in the silence nothing was to be heard save the drip-drip of Dutchy's spilled coffee on the floor. Dennin threw open the breech of the shot-gun, ejecting the empty shells. Holding the gun with one hand, he reached with the other into his pocket for fresh shells.

He was thrusting the shells into the gun when Edith Nelson was aroused to action. It was patent that he intended to kill Hans and her. For a space of possibly three seconds of time she had been dazed and paralysed by the horrible and inconceivable form in which the unexpected had made its appearance. Then she rose to it and grappled with it. She grappled with it concretely, making a cat-like leap for the murderer and gripping his neck-cloth with both her hands. The impact of her body sent him stumbling backward several steps. He tried to shake her loose and still retain his hold on the gun. This was awkward, for her firm-fleshed body had become a cat's. She threw herself to one side, and with her grip at his throat nearly jerked him to the floor. He straightened himself and whirled swiftly. Still faithful to her hold, her body followed the circle of his whirl so that her feet left the floor, and she swung through the air fastened to his throat by her hands. The whirl culminated in a collision with a chair, and the man and woman crashed to the floor in a wild struggling fall that extended itself across half the length of the room.

Hans Nelson was half a second behind his wife in rising to the unexpected. His nerve processed and mental processes were slower than hers. His was the grosser organism, and it had taken him half a second longer to perceive, and determine, and proceed to do. She had already flown at Dennin and gripped his throat, when Hans sprang to his feet. But her coolness was not his. He was in a blind fury, a Berserker rage. At the instant he sprang from his chair his mouth opened and there issued forth a sound that was half roar, half bellow. The whirl of the two bodies had already started, and still roaring, or bellowing, he pursued this whirl down the room, overtaking it when it fell to the floor.

Hans hurled himself upon the prostrate man, striking madly with his fists. They were sledge-like blows, and when Edith felt Dennin's body relax she loosed her grip and rolled clear. She lay on the floor, panting and watching. The fury of blows continued to rain down. Dennin did not seem to mind the blows. He did not even move. Then it dawned upon her that he was unconscious.

She cried out to Hans to stop. She cried out again. But he paid no heed to her voice. She caught him by the arm, but her clinging to it merely impeded his effort.

It was no reasoned impulse that stirred her to do what she then did. Nor was it a sense of pity, nor obedience to the "Thou shalt not" of religion. Rather was it some sense of law, an ethic of her race and early environment, that compelled her to interpose her body between her husband and the helpless murderer. It was not until Hans knew he was striking his wife that he ceased. He allowed himself to be shoved away by her in much the same way that a ferocious but obedient dog allows itself to be shoved away by its master. The analogy went even farther. Deep in his throat, in an animal-like way, Hans's rage still rumbled, and several times he made as though to spring back upon his prey and was only prevented by the woman's swiftly interposed body.

Back and farther back Edith shoved her husband. She had never seen him in such a condition, and she was more frightened of him than she had been of Dennin in the thick of the struggle. She could not believe that this raging beast was her Hans, and

with a shock she
became suddenly
aware of a shrinking,
instinctive fear that
he might snap her
hand in his teeth
like any wild animal.
For some seconds,
unwilling to hurt
her, yet dogged in
his desire to return
to the attack,
Hans dodged back
and forth. But she
resolutely dodged
with him, until the

first glimmerings of reason returned and he gave over.

Both crawled to their feet. Hans staggered back against the wall, where he leaned, his face working, in his throat the deep and continuous rumble that died away with the seconds and at last ceased. The time for the reaction had come. Edith stood in the middle of the floor, wringing her hands, panting and gasping, her whole body trembling violently.

Hans looked at nothing, but Edith's eyes wandered wildly from detail to detail of what had taken place. Dennin lay without movement. The overturned chair,

hurled onward in the
mad whirl, lay near
him. Partly under
him lay the shot-gun,
still broken open at
the breech. Spilling
out of his right
hand were the two
cartridges which he
had failed to put into
the gun and which
he had clutched
until consciousness
left him. Harkey
lay on the floor,
face downward,

where he had fallen; while Dutchy rested forward on the table, his yellow mop of hair buried in his mush-plate, the plate itself still tilted at an angle of forty-five degrees. This tilted plate fascinated her. Why did it not fall down? It was ridiculous. It was not in the nature of things for a mush-plate to up-end itself on the table, even if a man or so had been killed.

She glanced back at Dennin, but her eyes returned to the tilted plate. It was so ridiculous! She felt a hysterical impulse to laugh. Then she noticed the silence, and forgot the plate in a desire for something to happen. The monotonous drip of the coffee from the table to the floor merely emphasized the silence. Why did not Hans do something? say something? She looked at him and was about to speak, when she discovered that her tongue refused its wonted duty. There was a peculiar ache in her throat, and her mouth was dry and furry.

She could only look at Hans, who, in turn, looked at her.

Suddenly the silence was broken by a sharp, metallic clang. She screamed, jerking her eyes back to the table. The plate had fallen down. Hans sighed as though awakening from sleep. The clang of the plate had aroused them to life in a new world. The cabin epitomized the new world in which they must thenceforth live and move. The old cabin was gone forever. The horizon of life was totally new and unfamiliar. The unexpected had swept its wizardry over the face of things, changing the perspective, juggling values, and shuffling the real and the unreal into perplexing confusion.

"My God, Hans!" was Edith's first speech.

He did not answer, but stared at her with horror. Slowly his eyes wandered over the room, for the first time taking in its details. Then he put on his cap and started for the door.

"Where are you going?" Edith demanded, in an agony of apprehension.

His hand was on the door-knob, and he half turned as he answered, "To dig some graves."

"Don't leave me, Hans, with—" her eyes swept the room—"with this."

“The graves must be dug sometime,” he said.

“But you do not know how many,” she objected desperately. She noted his indecision, and added, “Besides, I’ll go with you and help.”

Hans stepped back to the table and mechanically snuffed the candle.

Then between them they made the examination. Both Harkey and Dutchy were dead—frightfully dead, because of the close range of the shot-gun. Hans refused to go near Dennin, and Edith was forced to conduct this portion of the investigation by herself.

"He isn't dead," she called to Hans.

He walked over and looked down at the murderer.

"What did you say?" Edith demanded, having caught the rumble of inarticulate speech in her husband's throat.

"I said it was a damn shame that he isn't

dead," came the reply.

Edith was bending over the body.

"Leave him alone," Hans commanded harshly, in a strange voice.

She looked at him in sudden alarm. He had picked up the shot-gun dropped by Dennin and was thrusting in the shells.

"What are you going to do?" she cried, rising swiftly from her bending position.

Hans did not answer, but she saw the shot-gun going to his shoulder. She grasped the muzzle with her hand and threw it up.

“Leave me alone!” he cried hoarsely.

He tried to jerk the weapon away from her, but she came in closer and clung to him.

“Hans! Hans! Wake up!” she cried. “Don’t be crazy!”

“He killed Dutchy and Harkey!” was her husband’s reply; “and

I am going to kill him."

"But that is wrong," she objected. "There is the law."

He sneered his incredulity of the law's potency in such a region, but he merely iterated, dispassionately, doggedly, "He killed Dutchy and Harkey."

Long she argued
it with him, but
the argument was
one-sided, for he
contented himself
with repeating again
and again, "He killed
Dutchy and Harkey."
But she could not
escape from her
childhood training
nor from the blood
that was in her.
The heritage of law
was hers, and right
conduct, to her, was

the fulfilment of the law. She could see no other righteous course to pursue. Hans's taking the law in his own hands was no more justifiable than Dennin's deed. Two wrongs did not make a right, she contended, and there was only one way to punish Dennin, and that was the legal way arranged by society. At last Hans gave in to her.

“All right,” he said. “Have it your own way. And to-morrow or next day look to see him kill you and me.”

She shook her head and held out her hand for the shot-gun. He started to hand it to her, then hesitated.

"Better let me shoot him," he pleaded.

Again she shook her head, and again he started to pass her the gun, when the door opened, and an Indian, without knocking, came in. A blast of wind and flurry of snow came in with him. They turned and faced him, Hans still holding the shot-gun.

The intruder took in the scene without a quiver. His eyes embraced the dead and wounded in a sweeping glance. No surprise showed in his face, not even curiosity. Harkey lay at his feet, but he took no notice of him. So far as he was concerned, Harkey's body did not exist.

"Much wind," the Indian remarked by way of salutation. "All well? Very well?"

Hans, still grasping the gun, felt sure that the Indian attributed to him the mangled corpses. He glanced appealingly at his wife.

"Good morning, Negook," she said, her voice betraying her effort. "No, not very well. Much trouble."

"Good-by, I go now, much hurry," the Indian said, and without semblance of haste, with great deliberation stepping clear of a red pool on the floor, he opened the door and went out.

The man and woman looked at each other.

"He thinks we did it," Hans gasped, "that I did it."

Edith was silent for a space. Then she said, briefly, in a businesslike way:

"Never mind what he thinks. That will come after. At present we have two graves to dig. But first of all, we've got to tie up Dennin so he can't escape."

Hans refused to touch Dennin, but Edith lashed him securely, hand and foot. Then she and Hans went out into the snow. The ground was frozen. It was impervious to a blow of the pick. They first gathered wood, then scraped the snow away and on the frozen surface built a fire. When the fire had burned for an hour, several inches of dirt had thawed. This they shovelled out, and then built a fresh fire. Their descent into the earth progressed at the rate of two or three inches an hour.

It was hard and bitter work. The flurrying snow did not permit the fire to burn any too well, while the wind cut through their clothes and chilled their bodies. They held but little conversation. The wind interfered with speech. Beyond wondering at what could have been Dennin's motive, they remained silent, oppressed by the horror of the tragedy. At one o'clock, looking toward the cabin, Hans announced that he was hungry.

"No, not now, Hans," Edith answered. "I couldn't go back alone into that cabin the way it is, and cook a meal."

At two o'clock Hans volunteered to go with her; but she held him to his work, and four o'clock found the two graves completed. They were shallow, not more than two feet deep, but they would serve the purpose. Night had fallen. Hans got the sled, and the two dead men were dragged through the darkness and storm to their frozen sepulchre. The funeral procession was anything but a pageant. The sled sank deep into the drifted snow and pulled hard. The man and the woman had eaten nothing since the previous day, and were weak from hunger and exhaustion. They had not the strength to resist the wind, and at times its buffets hurled them off their feet. On several occasions the sled was overturned, and they were compelled to reload it with its sombre freight. The last hundred feet to the graves was up a steep slope, and this they took on all fours, like sled-dogs, making legs of their arms and thrusting their hands into the snow. Even so, they were twice dragged backward by the weight of the sled, and slid and fell down the hill, the living and the dead, the haul-ropes and the sled, in ghastly entanglement.

"To-morrow I will put up head-boards with their names," Hans said, when the graves were filled in.

Edith was sobbing. A few broken sentences had been all she was capable of in the way of a funeral service, and now her husband was compelled to half-carry her back to the cabin.

Dennin was conscious. He had rolled over and over on the floor in vain efforts to free himself. He watched Hans and Edith with glittering eyes, but made no attempt to speak. Hans still refused to touch the murderer, and sullenly watched Edith drag him across the floor to the men's bunk-room. But try as she would, she could not lift him from the floor into his bunk.

"Better let me shoot him, and we'll have no more trouble," Hans said in final appeal.

Edith shook her head and bent again to her

task. To her surprise the body rose easily, and she knew Hans had relented and was helping her. Then came the cleansing of the kitchen.
But the floor still shrieked the tragedy, until Hans planed the surface of the stained wood away and with the shavings made a fire in the stove.

The days came and went. There was much of darkness and silence, broken only by the storms and the thunder on the beach of the freezing surf. Hans was obedient to Edith's slightest order. All his splendid initiative had vanished. She had elected to deal with Dennin in her way, and so he left the whole matter in her hands.

The murderer was a constant menace. At all times there was the chance that he might free himself from his bonds, and they were compelled to guard him day and night. The man or the woman sat always beside him, holding the loaded shot-gun. At first, Edith tried eight-hour watches, but the continuous strain was too great, and afterwards she and Hans relieved each other every four hours. As they had to sleep, and as the watches extended through the night, their whole waking time was expended in guarding Dennin. They had barely time left over for the preparation of meals and the getting of firewood.

Since Negook's inopportune visit, the Indians had avoided the cabin. Edith sent Hans to their cabins to get them to take Dennin down the coast in a canoe to the nearest white settlement or trading post, but the errand was fruitless. Then Edith went herself and interviewed Negook. He was head man of the little village, keenly aware of his responsibility, and he elucidated his policy thoroughly in few words.

"It is white man's trouble," he said, "not Siwash trouble. My people help you, then will it be Siwash trouble too. When white man's trouble and Siwash trouble come together and make a trouble, it is a great trouble, beyond understanding and without end. Trouble no good. My people do no wrong. What for they help you and have trouble?"

So Edith Nelson went back to the terrible cabin with its endless alternating four-hour watches.

Sometimes, when it was her turn and she sat by the prisoner, the loaded shot-gun in her lap, her eyes would close and she would doze. Always she aroused with a start, snatching up the gun and swiftly looking at him. These were distinct nervous shocks, and their effect was not good on her. Such was her fear of the man, that even though she were wide awake, if he moved under the bedclothes she could not repress the start and the quick reach for the gun.

She was preparing herself for a nervous break-down, and she knew it. First came a fluttering of the eyeballs, so that she was compelled to close her eyes for relief. A little later the eyelids were afflicted by a nervous twitching that she could not control. To add to the strain, she could not forget the tragedy. She remained as close to the horror as on the first morning when the unexpected stalked into the cabin and took possession. In her daily ministrations upon the prisoner she was forced to grit her teeth and steel herself, body and spirit.

Hans was affected differently. He became obsessed by the idea that it was his duty to kill Dennin; and whenever he waited upon the bound man or watched by him, Edith was troubled by the fear that Hans would add another red entry to the cabin's record. Always he cursed Dennin savagely and handled him roughly. Hans tried to conceal his homicidal mania, and he would say to his wife: "By and by you will want me to kill him, and then I will not kill him. It would make me sick." But more than once, stealing into the room, when it was her watch off, she would catch the two men glaring ferociously at each other, wild animals the pair of them, in Hans's face the lust to kill, in Dennin's the fierceness and savagery of the cornered rat. "Hans!" she would cry, "wake up!" and he would come to a recollection of himself, startled and shamefaced and unrepentant.

So Hans became another factor in the problem the unexpected had given Edith Nelson to solve. At first it had been merely a question of right conduct in dealing with Dennin, and right conduct, as she conceived it, lay in keeping him a prisoner until he could be turned over for trial before a proper tribunal. But now entered Hans, and she saw that his sanity and his salvation were involved. Nor was she long in discovering that her own strength and endurance had become part of the problem. She was breaking down under the strain. Her left arm had developed involuntary jerkings and twitchings. She spilled her food from her spoon, and could place no reliance in her afflicted arm. She judged it to be a form of St. Vitus's dance, and she feared the extent to which its ravages might go. What if she broke down? And the vision she had of the possible future, when the cabin might contain only Dennin and Hans, was an added horror.

After the third day, Dennin had begun to talk. His first question had been, "What are you going to do with me?" And this question he repeated daily and many times a day. And always Edith replied that he would assuredly be dealt with according to law. In turn, she put a daily question to him,—“Why did you do it?” To this he never replied. Also, he received the question with out-bursts of anger, raging and straining at the rawhide that bound him and threatening her with what he would do when he got loose, which he said he was sure to do sooner or later. At such times she cocked both triggers of the gun, prepared to meet him with leaden death if he should burst loose, herself trembling and palpitating and dizzy from the tension and shock.

But in time Dennin grew more tractable. It seemed to her that he was growing weary of his unchanging recumbent position. He began to beg and plead to be released. He made wild promises. He would do them no harm. He would himself go down the coast and give himself up to the officers of the law. He would give them his share of the gold. He would go away into the heart of the wilderness, and never again appear in civilization. He would take his own life if she would only free him. His pleadings usually culminated in involuntary raving, until it seemed to her that he was passing into a fit; but always she shook her head and denied him the freedom for which he worked himself into a passion.

But the weeks went by, and he continued to grow more tractable. And through it all the weariness was asserting itself more and more. "I am so tired, so tired," he would murmur, rolling

his head back and
forth on the pillow
like a peevish child.
At a little later period
he began to make
impassioned pleas for
death, to beg her to
kill him, to beg Hans
to put him our of his
misery so that he
might at least rest
comfortably.

The situation was
fast becoming
impossible. Edith's

nervousness was increasing, and she knew her break-down might come any time. She could not even get her proper rest, for she was haunted by the fear that Hans would yield to his mania and kill Dennin while she slept. Though January had already come, months would have to elapse before any trading schooner was even likely to put into the bay. Also, they had not expected to winter in the cabin, and the food was running low; nor could Hans add to the supply by hunting. They were chained to the cabin by the necessity of guarding their prisoner.

Something must be done, and she knew

it. She forced herself to go back into a reconsideration of the problem. She could not shake off the legacy of her race, the law that was of her blood and that had been trained into her. She knew that whatever she did she must do according to the law, and in the long hours of watching, the shot-gun on her knees, the murderer restless beside her and the storms thundering without, she made original sociological researches and worked out for herself the evolution of the law. It came to her that the law was nothing more than the judgment and the will of any group of people. It mattered not how large was the group of people. There were little groups, she reasoned, like Switzerland, and there were big groups like the United States. Also, she reasoned, it did not matter how small was the group of people. There might be only ten thousand people in a country, yet their collective judgment and will would be the law of that country. Why, then, could not one thousand people constitute such a group? she asked herself. And if one thousand, why not one hundred? Why not fifty? Why not five? Why not—two?

She was frightened at her own conclusion, and she talked it over with Hans. At first he could not comprehend, and then, when he did, he added convincing evidence. He spoke of miners' meetings, where all the men of a locality came together and made the law and executed the law. There might be only ten or fifteen men altogether, he said, but the will of the majority became the law for the whole ten or fifteen, and whoever violated that will was punished.

Edith saw her way clear at last. Dennin must hang. Hans agreed with her. Between them they constituted the majority of this particular group. It was the group-will that Dennin should be hanged. In the execution of this will Edith strove earnestly to observe the customary forms, but the group was so small that Hans and she had to serve as witnesses, as jury, and as judges—also as executioners. She formally charged Michael Dennin with the murder of Dutchy and Harkey, and the prisoner lay in his bunk and listened to the testimony, first of Hans, and then of Edith. He refused to plead guilty or not guilty, and remained silent when she asked him if he had anything to say in his own defence. She and Hans, without leaving their seats, brought in the jury's verdict of guilty. Then, as judge, she imposed the sentence. Her voice shook, her eyelids twitched, her left arm jerked, but she carried it out.

"Michael Dennin, in three days' time you are to be hanged by the neck until you are dead."

Such was the sentence. The man breathed an unconscious sigh of relief, then laughed defiantly, and said, "Thin I'm thinkin' the damn bunk won't be achin' me back anny more, an' that's a consolation."

With the passing of the sentence a feeling of relief seemed to communicate itself to all of them. Especially was it noticeable in Dennin. All sullenness and defiance disappeared, and he talked sociably with his captors, and even with flashes of his old-time wit. Also, he found great satisfaction in Edith's reading to him from the Bible. She read from the New Testament, and he took keen interest in the prodigal son and the thief on the cross.

On the day preceding that set for the

execution, when Edith asked her usual question, “Why did you do it?” Dennin answered, “’Tis very simple. I was thinkin’—”

But she hushed him abruptly, asked him to wait, and hurried to Hans’s bedside. It was his watch off, and he came out of his sleep, rubbing his eyes and grumbling.

"Go," she told him, "and bring up Negook and one other Indian. Michael's going to confess. Make them come. Take the rifle along and bring them up at the point of it if you have to."

Half an hour later Negook and his uncle, Hadikwan, were ushered into the death chamber. They came unwillingly,

Hans with his rifle herding them along.

“Negook,” Edith said, “there is to be no trouble for you and your people. Only is it for you to sit and do nothing but listen and understand.”

Thus did Michael Dennin, under sentence of death, make public confession of his crime. As he talked,

Edith wrote his story down, while the Indians listened, and Hans guarded the door for fear the witnesses might bolt.

He had not been home to the old country for fifteen years, Dennin explained, and it had always been his intention to return with plenty of money and make his old mother comfortable for the rest of her days.

"An' how was I to be doin' it on sixteen hundred?" he demanded. "What I was after wantin' was all the goold, the whole eight thousan'. Thin I cud go back in style. What ud be aisier, thinks I to myself, than to kill all iv yez, report it at Skaguay for an Indian-killin', an' thin pull out for Ireland? An' so I started in to kill all iv yez, but, as Harkey was fond of sayin', I cut out too large a chunk an' fell down on the swallowin' iv it. An' that's me confession. I did me duty to the devil, an' now, God willin', I'll do me duty to God."

"Negook and Hadikwan, you have heard the white man's words," Edith said to the Indians. "His words are here on this paper, and it is for you to make a sign, thus, on the paper, so that white men to come after will know that you have heard."

The two Siwashes put crosses opposite

their signatures, received a summons to appear on the morrow with all their tribe for a further witnessing of things, and were allowed to go.

Dennin's hands were released long enough for him to sign the document. Then a silence fell in the room. Hans was restless, and Edith felt uncomfortable. Dennin lay on his back, staring straight up at the moss-chinked roof.

“An’ now I’ll do me duty to God,” he murmured. He turned his head toward Edith. “Read to me,” he said, “from the book;” then added, with a glint of playfulness, “Mayhap

’twill help me to forget the bunk.”

The day of the execution broke clear and cold. The thermometer was down to twenty-five below zero, and a chill wind was blowing which drove the frost through clothes and flesh to the bones. For the first time in many weeks Dennin stood upon his feet. His muscles had remained inactive so long, and he was so out of practice in maintaining an erect position, that he could scarcely stand.

He reeled back and forth, staggered, and clutched hold of Edith with his bound hands for support.

"Sure, an' it's dizzy I am," he laughed weakly.

A moment later he said, "An' it's glad I am that it's over with. That damn bunk would iv been the death iv me, I know."

When Edith put his fur cap on his head and proceeded to pull the flaps down over his ears, he laughed and said:

"What are you doin' that for?"

"It's freezing cold outside," she answered.

"An' in tin minutes' time what'll matter a frozen ear or so to poor Michael Dennin?" he asked.

She had nerved herself for the last culminating ordeal, and his remark was like a blow to her self-possession. So far, everything had seemed phantom-like, as in a dream, but the brutal truth of what he had said shocked her eyes wide open to the reality of what was taking place. Nor was her distress unnoticed by the Irishman.

“I’m sorry to be troublin’ you with me foolish spache,” he said regretfully. “I mint nothin’ by it. ’Tis a great day for Michael Dennin, an’ he’s as gay as a lark.”

He broke out in a merry whistle, which quickly became lugubrious and ceased.

“I’m wishin’ there was a priest,” he said wistfully; then added swiftly, “But Michael Dennin’s too old a campaigner to miss the luxuries when he hits the trail.”

He was so very weak and unused to walking that when the door opened and he passed outside, the wind nearly carried him off his feet. Edith and Hans walked on either side of him and supported him, the while he cracked jokes and tried to keep them cheerful, breaking off, once, long enough to arrange the forwarding of his share of the gold to his mother in Ireland.

They climbed a slight hill and came out into an open space among the trees. Here, circled solemnly about a barrel that stood on end in the snow, were Negook and Hadikwan, and all the Siwashes down to the babies and the dogs, come to see the way of the white man's law. Near by was an open grave which Hans had burned into the frozen earth.

Dennin cast a practical eye over the preparations, noting the grave, the barrel, the thickness of the rope, and the diameter of the limb over which the rope was passed.

"Sure, an' I couldn't iv done better meself, Hans, if it'd been for you."

He laughed loudly at his own sally, but

Hans's face was frozen into a sullen ghastliness that nothing less than the trump of doom could have broken. Also, Hans was feeling very sick. He had not realized the enormousness of the task of putting a fellow-man out of the world. Edith, on the other hand, had realized; but the realization did not make the task any easier. She was filled with doubt as to whether she could hold herself together long enough to finish it. She felt incessant impulses to scream, to shriek, to collapse into the snow, to put her hands over her eyes and turn and run blindly away, into the forest, anywhere, away. It was only by a supreme effort of soul that she was able to keep upright and go on and do what she had to do. And in the midst of it all she was grateful to Dennin for the way he helped her.

"Lind me a hand," he said to Hans, with whose assistance he managed to mount the barrel.

He bent over so that Edith could adjust

the rope about his neck. Then he stood upright while Hans drew the rope taut across the overhead branch.

"Michael Dennin, have you anything to say?" Edith asked in a clear voice that shook in spite of her.

Dennin shuffled his feet on the barrel, looked down bashfully like a man making his maiden speech, and cleared his throat.

"I'm glad it's over with," he said. "You've treated me like a Christian, an' I'm thankin' you hearty for your kindness."

"Then may God receive you, a repentant sinner," she said.

"Ay," he answered, his deep voice as a response to her thin one, "may God receive me, a repentant sinner."

"Good-by, Michael," she cried, and her voice sounded desperate.

She threw her weight against the barrel, but it did not overturn.

"Hans! Quick! Help me!" she cried faintly.

She could feel her last strength going, and the barrel resisted her. Hans hurried to her, and the barrel went out from under Michael Dennin.

She turned her back, thrusting her fingers into her ears. Then she began to laugh, harshly, sharply, metallically; and Hans was shocked as he had not been shocked through the whole tragedy. Edith Nelson's break-down had come. Even in her hysteria she knew it, and she was glad that she had been able to hold up under the strain until everything had been accomplished. She reeled toward Hans.

“Take me to the cabin, Hans,” she managed to articulate.

“And let me rest,” she added. “Just let me rest, and rest, and rest.”

With Hans’s arm around her, supporting her weight and directing her helpless steps, she went off across the snow. But the Indians remained solemnly to watch the working of the white man's law that compelled a man to dance upon the air.

ABOUT THE AUTHOR

Jack London went to the Klondike during the gold rush boom. He developed scurvy, lost his front four teeth, and injured his leg. He then decided to "sell his brains". He saw his writing as a business, his ticket out of poverty, and a way of beating the wealthy at their own game.

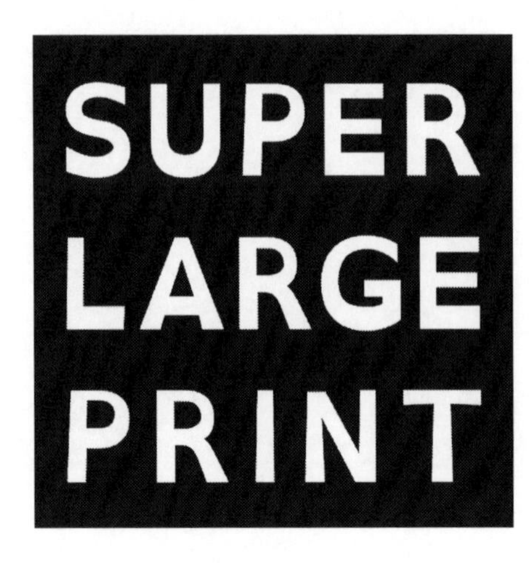

MORE BOOKS AT:

superlargeprint.com

KEEP ON READING!

This book is set in a font designed by Abelardo Gonzalez called OpenDyslexic

ISBN 9798689941752

Printed in Great Britain
by Amazon